THE WORLD
OF CHAOS

MURO
THE RAT
MONSTER

With special thanks to Thea Bennett

To Oliver and Zoë

www.beastquest.co.uk

ORCHARD BOOKS
338 Euston Road, London NW1 3BH
Orchard Books Australia
Level 17/207 Kent St, Sydney, NSW 2000

A Paperback Original
First published in Great Britain in 2010

Beast Quest is a registered trademark of Working Partners Limited
Series created by Beast Quest Limited, London

Text © Beast Quest Limited 2010
Cover illustration by Steve Sims © Orchard Books 2010
Inside illustrations by Ovi@kja-artists.com © Orchard Books 2010

A CIP catalogue record for this book is available from
the British Library.

ISBN 978 1 40830 724 3

9 10

Printed and bound by CPI Group (UK) Ltd, CR0 4YY

The paper and board used in this paperback are natural recyclable
products made from wood grown in sustainable forests. The
manufacturing processes conform to the environmental regulations of
the country of origin.

Orchard Books is a division of Hachette Children's Books,
an Hachette UK company.

www.hachette.co.uk

MurO
THE RAT
MONSTER

BY ADAM BLADE

ORCHARD

Hail, young warriors!

Tom has set out on a Quest of his own choosing, and I have the honour of helping with magic learnt from the greatest teacher of them all: my master, Aduro. Tom's challenges will be great: a new kingdom, a lost mother and six more Beasts under Velmal's spell. Tom isn't just fighting to save a kingdom. He's fighting to save those lives closest to him and to prove that love can conquer evil. Can it? Tom will only find out by staying strong and keeping the flame of hope alive. As long as no foul wind blows it out...

Yours truly,

The apprentice, Marc

PROLOGUE

The hot sun shone down on the
golden cornfields of the Kayonian
Plain, the crops bending and swaying
at the command of a light breeze.

Roland gazed into the sky. The days
and nights were unpredictable in
Kayonia, and the sun could set at
any moment.

I'd better get moving, he thought.

Across the vast cornfields, other

farmers were gathering their share of the crop. Roland didn't want to lag behind.

He had seen many harvests, but this seemed to be the best in years. The ears of corn carried plump grains. When these kernels were ground at the village windmill, they would make flour that the villagers could sell.

Roland raised his crescent-shaped scythe. He sang an ancient harvest song to himself as the blade sliced through the cornstalks. *"Hey-yah! The day is soon done! Hey-yah! Let us work while we can, for the sun is soon gone!"*

The corn fell at his feet as he walked through the field, swinging the scythe.

"Urgh!" Roland suddenly choked. A foul, rotting stench caught at the back of his throat. He looked around.

He saw nothing except a sea of golden corn.

A rustling disturbed the cornstalks. It sounded like the mice that plagued the grain stores in the village – but much, *much* louder.

Something jumped out of the corn and landed on Roland's foot. It was a fat grey rat, staring at him with beady red eyes.

Roland shooed the rat away. He shuddered as more of the mangy creatures appeared. His skin crawled at the sight of their naked tails and long brown claws.

"They're only rats!" he told himself. Roland swung his scythe, and the rats scurried away. But the horrible smell lingered. He saw that in some places the cornstalks had been eaten away and were covered in slimy black mildew.

"This crop is diseased!" he said, with a groan of despair. Perhaps the harvest was not going to be such a good one, after all. He must tell the other villagers, so they could act quickly and save the crops.

He grabbed an armful of the corn he'd cut, tied it into a sheaf, and hoisted it onto his shoulder. As he straightened up, a loud, whistling shriek echoed across the cornfields.

The sound made his scalp prickle. The ground vibrated beneath him, as if pounded by heavy hooves. Then he glimpsed the humped back of a large animal looming above the corn, heading his way.

One of the bulls has escaped! he thought, as the humped back dipped and rose with the creature's great pace.

But no bull can run that fast! When the creature appeared before him, he realised it was not a bull – it was like nothing he had ever seen before. Roland's mouth fell open as he saw a pointed, whiskery face. It was a giant rat! Its dark hide was thick with matted, patchy fur. Its long nose twitched below evil red eyes.

Roland dropped his sheaf and ran along the path that he had cut through the corn.

"Help me! Please!" he shouted, fear bringing bile into his throat. But the other farmers were too far away, harvesting their own crops.

No one could hear him.

Roland reached his cart where he had stacked all the harvested sheaves. He flung himself underneath and held his breath. All he could hear was the thudding of his heart. The ground began to shake. Four huge paws approached the cart at speed, each ending with twisted yellow claws.

The Beast crashed into the cart and Roland screamed. The giant rat charged again and the cart toppled onto its side.

Exposed, the helpless farmer gazed up. The sun was setting and the Beast's evil eyes glowed blood-red. Roland choked on the foul smell of the drool that dripped from its long yellow teeth.

The jagged teeth closed in on Roland's face. He tried to scream again, but no sound escaped his lips. The cornfields were plunged into darkness, and the Kayonian farmer knew nothing more.

CHAPTER ONE

JOURNEY INTO DANGER

Tom woke up and rubbed his eyes. He felt as if he had only just fallen asleep, but already the sun was high over the icy Kayonian desert.

Elenna was lying a few feet away, wrapped in a thick, quilted cloak.

"Elenna! Wake up!" he called.

Tom's companion rolled over and yawned. "Brrr! It's really cold," she said. "What's happened to our fire?"

Tom looked at the remains of the campfire from the night before. Beyond the pile of embers, the black sand of the desert stretched away, glittering with ice crystals. The firewood was a parting gift from the tribe of nomads they had helped after the previous Quest against Komodo the lizard king: the Black Cactus he had harvested had healed their horses' diseased hooves.

"We need to get going," Tom said to Elenna. "We don't know how long the daylight will last."

Tom had to get the next ingredient for the magic potion that would save his mother, Freya, from Velmal's clutches. He felt sadness wash over him as he thought of her. Freya was Mistress of the Beasts from the great kingdom of Gwildor, but all her power was lost. Now she was weak and ill from Velmal's poison.

Tom picked up his stallion's saddle. Storm stood by the remains of the campfire, dozing with his head bowed low. Nearby, Silver the wolf was stretched out on the cold sand, his thick fur keeping him warm.

Suddenly, the wolf sprang to his feet, barking as smoke rose up from the ashes of the fire.

"Look, Tom!" cried Elenna, as flames crackled and blazed.

Through the billowing smoke a face appeared, grinning at Tom from under a floppy wizard's hat.

It was Marc, the young apprentice to the good wizard Aduro.

"Greetings, Tom and Elenna!" Marc said, stepping out of the fire. "You did well to recover the Black Cactus. Now your next Quest begins."

As well as helping the nomads' horses, the Black Cactus was the first ingredient for the magic potion that would cure Tom's mother. However, the potion needed six ingredients.

"I have come to warn you," said Marc. "The Beast you now face is the

deadliest foe yet. You must confront Muro the rat monster!"

Tom felt a tingle of excitement run through his veins.

"And what ingredient...?" Tom began.

But Marc's image was fading. "I cannot stay," he said, stepping back into the fire. "I am needed at Queen Romaine's castle! Velmal's strength is growing. Soon..." Marc vanished. The fire disappeared in a puff of smoke.

Tom felt cold with dread as he thought of his mother. If he lost her now, after he'd only just found her, he would never forgive himself.

Elenna put her hand on Tom's shoulder. "Let's find out where we must go," she said.

Tom reached for the amulet that

hung around his neck. Rays of light burst from it, and a map of the freezing desert glittered on its surface. Their route was marked with a bright red line.

Tom traced the path until it entered a wide flat land where tall crops grew. He felt his heart ache as he thought of the Grassy Plains of Avantia, near his home village of Errinel. He wished he were there now, lying on his back in the warm sunshine, listening to the wind softly rustling through the grass.

"Not yet!" he said to himself. "While there's blood in my veins, I will fight until Velmal is defeated!"

The twisting path flashed on the map. It had reached a black blot, which quivered with menacing energy: the target of their Quest.

Tom peered at the blurred shape. It had a huge body, like a bison, but with the pointed head of a huge rat! Underneath it, Tom could see the name MURO spelled out.

"A rat monster!" he said. His stomach knotted with apprehension.

Elenna shuddered. "Rats are one of the things that I really hate!"

"I can't see anything like an ingredient on the map," said Tom. "It must be hidden somewhere on the Beast's body."

The two friends cleared away the camp. Tom saddled Storm and leapt onto his back. Elenna vaulted up behind him.

They set off at a fast gallop. Silver raced beside them, barking with excitement at being on a new Quest.

Soon the air felt warmer on Tom's

face. The icy desert was giving way to fields.

"We're almost there!" he called to Elenna.

Elenna tugged at his shoulder. "Stop! Look at Silver!" she cried.

Tom pulled Storm to a halt. Silver ran up to them. He sniffed the air and whined, his nose wrinkling.

"He can smell something bad," said Elenna.

"Something must be happening in those cornfields," said Tom. "We're certainly heading the right way."

They set off again, this time at a steady trot. Silver padded alongside, looking warily ahead.

The sun's rays beat onto the top of Tom's head. Sweat ran down his back. Up ahead, golden cornfields stretched away as far as he could see.

Tom coughed as a gust of foul air hit him. A terrible smell of decay drifted from the fields. He held his sleeve over his nose.

"Where's it coming from?" asked Elenna, holding her scarf up to her face.

The only thing in sight was a windmill, its sails spinning briskly. Something about the windmill made Tom feel uneasy. Then he realised what it was.

The sails of the mill are moving, but the corn in the fields isn't! How are the sails spinning without any wind to power them?

He licked his finger and held it up. The air was still.

"There's something wrong here," he said. "And I think that windmill holds the key…"

CHAPTER TWO

THE HARVEST
OF DEATH

Tom dug his heels into Storm's
flanks, and the stallion cantered
boldly towards the cornfields. Silver
loped behind.

They plunged between the rustling
cornstalks. Storm's hooves sank into
the wet, black soil. Tom and Elenna
clung on as he lurched through the
furrows.

All across the fields were deep irrigation ditches carrying water to the crops. Storm came to a halt at the edge of one. Silver jumped over the muddy trench. A stink of decay rose from the stagnant water.

"Come on, boy!" cried Tom.

Storm leapt bravely over the ditch. As he landed, the stallion skidded, almost falling to the ground.

"We'd better dismount," said Tom. "He can't carry us through this mud."

Tom and Elenna slid off Storm's back. Silver padded over, panting hard. The corn waved high above their heads.

The windmill's sails were still whirring eerily round. Tom led the way towards it, squelching through the mud. Decaying corn roots tangled around their legs, threatening to trip them with every step.

"Why haven't the crops been harvested?" asked Elenna, pausing for breath. "This corn has just been left to rot!" She bent down to unwind a strand of slimy, rotting vegetation from her ankle.

As Tom waited for her, he heard a loud thumping noise coming from the direction of the windmill.

"What's that?" he said. "It sounds like a drum beating."

Elenna listened. "I can hear voices," she said.

Tom could just make out the words of a chanting song.

"*Hey mah, hoh mah. The corn must fall. Yey mah, yoh mah. So our people grow tall.*" the voices droned.

"It sounds like a harvest song," Tom said.

Elenna looked at the putrefying corn and frowned. "But the crops are diseased and dying," she said. "No one is harvesting them."

"Let's keep going," said Tom. "We need to find out what's wrong, and these people might have food to sell."

"We need water, too," said Elenna. "Our flasks are almost empty."

The friends stepped out of the field. Tom saw low white buildings with flat roofs clustering round the windmill. In the village square was a crowd of people wearing mud-coloured robes. Tom felt uneasy. Why were they standing so still?

"Let's stay close together," he said to Elenna.

They walked past the houses and entered the village square. Tom saw that the people were gathered round a huge cauldron, placed above a fire. They were chanting the harvest song in low, tired voices.

Many of them had bent backs, as if their robes were too heavy for them. No one looked at Tom and Elenna.

"What's the matter with them?" asked Elenna.

"I don't know," said Tom. "But I'm going to find out."

At the edge of the village, large tarpaulins were stretched out. They looked like the covers that protected the underground grain pits in Tom's village.

"Those must be the grain stores," he said to Elenna.

"And here's the water supply!" Elenna went over to a large iron pump.

Tom pulled out their water flasks so

she could fill them up. Elenna tugged at the pump handle.

"It doesn't work," she said.

Tom tried the handle. It was stuck. No water came out from the pump.

Silence fell in the square. The villagers stopped chanting and queued up by the cauldron. *Strange*, Tom thought. *None of them seemed to have noticed us*. A tall figure swathed in a long dark cloak was ladling out some kind of stew into bowls.

"Rotting crops and no water," Tom said, gazing round. "No wonder these people are forced to queue for food." His stomach rumbled. "But we need something to eat, too, or we won't be able to complete the Quest."

They hurried over. A thin man, with his face hidden by a hood, stood at the end of the line. He swayed backwards, bumping into Tom, almost knocking him over. Without a word of apology, the man moved forward again.

"He didn't even look round," whispered Elenna.

Silver sniffed at the villagers' cloaks. The fur on his back bristled as he growled.

"Steady, boy," Elenna said. "He doesn't mean any harm," she added, speaking to a woman nearby. The woman didn't respond. Silver padded away and stood next to Storm.

Tom and Elenna reached the front of the queue and waited eagerly for bowls of steaming stew.

The tall figure with the ladle was not thin and bent like the other villagers. His robes were made of a fine material with gleaming threads.

He passed a bowl to Elenna, who inhaled deeply over the stew.

"Smells delicious!" she said.

When the man reached down to serve the food, Tom saw how strong his arm muscles were.

As Tom reached out to take the food, there was a loud snarl. Silver was back! The wolf leapt forward, knocking the bowl to the ground. With bared teeth, he lunged at the cloaked figure.

The man staggered, dropping the ladle. His hood fell back, revealing long, red hair. Tom's blood ran cold as he recognised the cruel face that confronted him.

Velmal!

CHAPTER THREE

THE POISONED VILLAGE

The wizard threw back his head and laughed.

"Your friend is very hungry, Tom!" he jeered.

Elenna was holding the bowl to her lips.

"Don't eat it!" Tom shouted, knocking it from her hands. The stew spattered across the ground.

"It's poisoned. Velmal is destroying the crops and using his own food to bewitch the villagers. That's why they're behaving so strangely."

Elenna moved closer to Tom, and placed an arrow into her bow. Tom drew his sword. The other villagers didn't even stir.

The wizard's eyes glowed. "How clever you are!" he snarled. He lifted the edge of his robe and swirled it through the air. Tom felt his sword being pulled from his hand by Velmal's magic. It clattered away across the square.

"No!" cried Elenna, as her bow and arrow were also snatched from her grip. They hovered in the air for a moment before being flung to one side by the invisible force.

Velmal smiled. "The village is

completely under my control," he said. "And soon the rest of Kayonia will follow!"

Tom's face grew hot with anger. "Never!" he retorted. "We're fighting on the side of the warrior queen, and we will defeat you!" He rushed away and picked up his sword, his fingers tightening round the hilt.

A sneer twisted Velmal's face. "You think you can win?" he said. "Remember, one Mistress of the Beasts has already fallen prey to me!"

Tom's heart lurched. "Don't speak of my mother like that!" he cried. He pointed his sword blade at the wizard's heart. "I challenge you, Velmal, to face me in combat!"

The wizard's eyes narrowed to slits. "So, you dare to confront me," he muttered. He turned to the villagers and raised his arm.

"Awake, slaves!" shouted Velmal. At the sound of his harsh voice, the heads of the villagers snapped up. Moving as one, they turned to stare at Tom.

Tom gasped. Upon seeing the villagers' pale faces, his skin prickled with horror. Their eyes were blank, without pupils, and bright blue.

"Is there no limit to your evil, Velmal?" Tom cried.

Velmal cackled, turned his back on Tom and walked away.

"Stop!" Tom shouted. He raced after Velmal and struck at the wizard's head with his sword. Velmal stepped aside, evading the blow. He raised his hand.

"Tom, look out!" shouted Elenna.

A current of air blasted through

Tom's hair, tugging at his clothes – he was being pushed backwards! He fought against the gusting wind and ran at Velmal again, using all his strength to leap at the wizard.

Velmal flicked his wrist. This time Tom was caught in mid-jump. He was frozen, hanging in the air like a puppet.

I must be able to free myself! thought Tom. He focused his mind on his limbs, forcing them to move. He managed to shift his arm a fraction, making his shoulder muscles burn in agony. Sweat broke out on his face with the effort. It was no use. He was trapped by Velmal's spell.

"Pathetic!" said Velmal, shaking with laughter.

Tom twisted helplessly in the air. With a mocking laugh, the wizard

turned away and vanished.

Tom fell hard on his knees. He
gritted his teeth against the pain and
looked for his companions. He heard
Elenna shouting.

"Get back!" she yelled.

The villagers stood in a circle

around Elenna and the animals, staring with their empty blue eyes. She hadn't managed to retrieve her bow and arrow.

Tom raced over to help but a burly man grabbed him by the shoulder.

"Stop, traitor!" he said, in a heavy voice.

Tom shook off the man's hand. "I'm no traitor."

The man fixed Tom with his expressionless gaze. "You have committed treason against our ruler."

Tom didn't want to use his sword. This man wasn't the enemy. "You're wrong!" he said. "We're fighting on the side of *your* warrior queen!"

There was an angry murmur from the crowd. Several of the men and women hissed. Elenna was turning this way and that as the villagers closed in. Silver barked angrily at her feet.

The man spoke again. "We do not recognise any queen. *Velmal* is our saviour!"

The villagers chanted as they heard the wizard's name. "Velmal! Velmal!"

Tom tried to explain. "Velmal is no saviour," he said. "He is evil. He has cast a spell over you..."

No one listened. Storm neighed, rearing up as a villager seized his reins.

Tom managed to free himself, but another villager tripped him up, sending him sprawling. Before he could right himself, a hand seized his collar and another twisted the sword from his wrist.

"Traitor! Traitor!" shouted the crowd.

"Tom!" Elenna's voice was desperate.

A burly villager in a brown cloak had gripped her by the hair, pulling her head back against his chest.

Tom's blood ran cold as he saw the man was holding a rusty knife to her throat.

CHAPTER FOUR

THE DUNGEON PIT

Elenna's eyes were wide with fear.

"Let her go!" Tom shouted.

Silver sprang at the attacker, but he kicked him off and held Elenna so that her body shielded him from the wolf.

Tom fought against the man who held him as he tried to drag him across the village square, kicking him in the knee; he went down with a yelp.

But before Tom could escape, four more villagers seized Tom's arms.

"Get off me!" shouted Tom, struggling in their firm grasp.

"To jail with them!" yelled Elenna's captor, his sinister blue eyes gleaming. "Let them suffer with the others who plot against Kayonia!" He lowered his knife hand and shoved Elenna forwards.

"Hey!" shouted Tom.

The villagers pulled him and Elenna towards the edge of the square. Tom tried to fight his way free but there were too many hands on him now. He could feel his flesh bruising as fingers squeezed tightly round his limbs. Through the crowd, he could just make out the flash of his sword catching sunlight as a Kayonian took it away, along with the rest of their weapons.

Elenna was kicking and fighting back, screaming protests, but the people were too strong and too determined. Silver barked angrily, but could not get closer; he was limping slightly from where he'd been kicked.

As a villager closed in on him, the wolf growled and bounded off, disappearing among the grass.

Two other men led Storm away towards the stables. Tom's stallion neighed and tossed his head slightly, but had the good sense not to struggle.

Tom could see that he and Elenna were being dragged towards one of the underground grain stores, which had a heavy iron grille over the entrance.

A grey-cloaked woman pulled out

a big iron key, slipped it into the lock and opened the grille. A gust of cold, dank air came up from the dark pit beneath.

Tom's heart sank as he looked down into the dungeon.

"Throw them in!" Tom was pushed and he plummeted into the dark. His hands and knees jarred with pain as he fell onto hard stone.

"Ow!" cried Elenna, as she landed beside him. Above them, the iron grille clanged shut. Tom peered into the darkness. The damp air felt cold on his face.

He could hear Elenna breathing, and then came a rustle of movement from further away. Instinctively, Tom balled his hands into fists; they were not alone in the dungeon!

"Who's there?" Tom called.

"Ha!" A sinister laugh echoed off the stones.

Tom blinked, struggling to see. After a moment, he saw the walls of a round chamber. He found Elenna's face, a pale oval in the gloom. She gripped Tom's shoulder, pointing towards the wall. "There!"

Tom turned and saw four bedraggled men, with long hair and beards. The whites of their eyes glinted in the shadows.

"Their eyes look normal – not bewitched like the other villagers," he whispered.

"What are you staring at?" growled one man.

The prisoners wore filthy, ragged tunics. Their scrawny limbs were caked with filth. The man who had spoken scrambled to his feet. He was

51

tall, with broad shoulders. His
expression was hostile.

Tom crouched, ready to defend
himself. "We're not your enemies,"
he said.

"How can we trust you?" the tall
man replied. "And how will we
survive, now that there are two

more mouths to feed?"

Another prisoner spoke up. "All we have is bread and rainwater, and little enough of that," he said, breaking into a hacking cough.

"We don't want your food," said Tom. "We need to get out of here."

A third prisoner laughed. "There's no escape," he said. "You'll rot in here, just like us."

Tom went over to the wall of the dungeon. He ran his fingertips over the surface; it was impossible to get a handhold. The smooth stones fitted together tightly, and were covered in slippery moss.

Elenna passed him something. "I snatched these from Storm's saddlebag before they caught me," she said. It was the pair of spiderweb gloves he had found in Gwildor, before he battled Rokk the walking mountain in a previous Beast Quest.

Tom's heart swelled with hope. He put on the sticky gloves and grasped the wall.

Swift as a spider, Tom climbed up. The magic was working! But as he reached out a hand to a slimy stone, he felt a wave of doubt flood through him and the fingers of the glove slowly peeled off the wall.

"No!" Tom cried as he fell back to the ground. He turned his hands over and inspected the gloves with a sigh.

Elenna came to kneel beside him.

"What went wrong?" she asked.

"Don't you remember?" Tom replied. "My emerald wouldn't work properly to heal the horses on the last Quest, either. Kayonia is not a kindred kingdom to Avantia or Gwildor. The magic is not as strong here."

"We told you there was no escape," the tall man said, his voice deep with despair. "None of us have been able to find a way out."

Tom looked round at the prisoner's pale, gaunt faces. "Why are you here?" he asked.

"I stole a cow, so my starving family could have milk," answered the man through his cough.

"It was steal or die!" said another, "Our farms and our crops were destroyed by Velmal and his Beasts."

Tom could see from the way their bones showed through their skin that the prisoners had probably been starving for a long time even before they were imprisoned. Velmal's evil had forced them to commit crimes in order to survive.

"Are you here because of Velmal, too?" Elenna asked the tall man.

"I'm from a land called Gorgonia," he replied. "Another evil wizard drove me from my country and into this place."

Malvel! thought Tom, shivering as he remembered his old enemy, and the dark realm that he ruled. This man must be one of the rebels from the rainforest of Gorgonia who had battled against Malvel. Would this man help them now?

The grey light slanting through the grille above them was fading – the sun was setting. Soon they would not be able to see anything at all.

"We have to get out!" Tom said. "We must defeat the Beast and find the next ingredient."

The Gorgonian shook his head. "How can you? You're on the inside and the key's out there," he said.

Tom's heart sank. Then one of the prisoners began to whistle in the growing darkness. The sound gave Tom an idea.

"Listen to that!" he whispered to Elenna. "I think there might be a way out of here, after all!"

CHAPTER FIVE

SILVER TO THE RESCUE

"How?" Elenna asked. She gestured to the Gorgonian. "He's right – we need the key. Lift me up, Tom. If we can see where the key is, we might be able to figure something out."

Tom knelt down and Elenna clambered onto his shoulders. He gripped her hands to keep her steady and stood up slowly. The bars of the grille were still some way above. She let go of Tom's hands and stretched up, tottering dangerously.

"I can't reach," she gasped.

"Let's make a human pyramid," said Tom. "We need a strong anchorman at the bottom."

The Gorgonian rebel came over. He knelt down on all fours, and Tom stood on his back. Then Elenna jumped up on Tom's shoulders again. Now she was right under the grille.

"Can you see anything?" asked Tom.

Elenna peered out. "The three moons are shining," she said. "I can see the key! There's a guard, sleeping on the ground – he's got it in his hand. It's hopeless."

"No, it's not," Tom said, his thoughts chasing after each other.

"This might be a job for a wolf…"

Elenna's eyes shone. "Of course!"
She gave a special whistle to call her
loyal animal companion. "I just hope
he didn't run too far."

They waited, but nothing happened.
Elenna whistled again.

"Keep trying!" said Tom, grasping Elenna's feet. Her weight pressed down on his shoulders. He forced his muscles to stay steady as he balanced on the Gorgonian's back.

The man grunted. "It's hard work, carrying the two of you," he said.

The prisoners crowded round. "We're weak from lack of food," the man with the cough said. "But we'll help if we can."

The men held onto Tom and Elenna, lifting some of the weight from the Gorgonian's back.

Tom heard the sound of paws padding above them.

"Clever boy," Elenna whispered. Silver stepped across the grille, placing one foot at a time on the iron bars.

Tom could see a piece of thick rope round Silver's neck. The end of it was frayed.

"He's bitten through it," said Elenna, reaching through the bars to stroke the wolf's head. She turned to Tom. "What shall we do?"

"Just wait," Tom said. "And be ready."

Seeing his mistress trapped made Silver agitated. He growled and pawed at the iron bars.

"What's he doing?" said the Gorgonian as Silver's growls got louder and more desperate. "He'll wake up the guard."

Tom's lips curled in a small smile. "Exactly…"

With a groan, the guard woke up, muttering confusedly as he looked in the direction of the grain pit. He got up and walked over, angrily shouting, "Be off, you stupid mutt! Go away."

Wait for it, Tom told himself as he saw the guard approach the pit. The guard was so intent on the wolf that he didn't notice Tom and Elenna balanced beneath the grille.

Silver continued to growl and paw at the bars, doing whatever he could to free his mistress.

"Go on!" the guard said. "Scram!"

"Now!" Tom shouted and Elenna reached up to grab the guard by the ankles. Surprised, the guard shouted in fear as he lost his balance. His face hit the iron bars with a dull *thunk*!

"He's out cold!" Elenna cheered.

"Good," Tom heard the Gorgonian man groan. "Get the key and open the grille. We can't hold you much longer!"

Elenna took the key from the guard and fitted it into the lock. It took both hands to twist the massive key and she winced as she heard the lock mechanism grind. They couldn't afford to alert any other guards.

"Who goes there?" called a voice.

Tom heard footsteps approaching. *Oh no*, he thought.

Silver howled and bounded away. A moment later, Tom heard the same voice shout, "Wolf! Go away!"

"Clever boy," said Elenna. "He's leading the guard away from us."

Tom flashed her a smile. "You taught him well."

With the coast clear, Elenna pushed the grille open.

She hauled herself out, taking deep gulps of the fresh air. The silent village square was bathed in moonlight.

Elenna leant over the edge of the pit and pulled Tom out. Together, they helped the prisoners out of the grain pit, one by one. The last prisoner was pulled up with a rope Elenna found by a nearby well. Two of the prisoners hugged each other and jumped up and down on the spot, clamping their hands over their faces to stop any cheers erupting from their mouths.

Tom led them all across the square. They crouched against the wall of one of the houses, hiding in the shadows.

Nearby, the rustling cornfields gleamed in the moonlight. The stench of decay drifted on the night breeze. The prisoners crowded close to Tom and Elenna. The Gorgonian grasped Tom's shoulder.

"Why did you look at each other when I spoke of Gorgonia?" he said.

"We've been there," said Tom.

The man looked surprised. "But Malvel holds all Gorgonia under his spell. I only just got out of there alive," he said.

Tom could tell that the Gorgonian was remembering his terrible ordeals against Malvel. "All is well in your country now," Tom told him. "Malvel has been vanquished."

The man let go of Tom's shoulder, his face alive with happiness. "That's good news," he said. Then he frowned and added: "But here in Kayonia, Velmal's power grows greater every day. Soon he will reign supreme."

"Not if I have anything to do with it!" said Tom.

The Gorgonian grasped Tom's hand. "I wish you luck."

The prisoners were moving restlessly.

"It's not safe for us to stay," one said. "Let's head for the fields."

"Join us!" said another, touching Tom's arm. "You helped us, let us help you."

Tom shook his head. "Go to your leader, the warrior queen," he said. "Pledge yourselves to help her overcome the peril that threatens your land!"

The prisoners muttered amongst themselves. They looked afraid.

"You can trust us," Tom said. "We want to see Velmal defeated and Kayonia freed. Your queen needs your help."

The men nodded. They shook Tom and Elenna's hands, thanking them. Then they slipped away towards the fields.

"What will happen if Velmal

catches them?" whispered Elenna, as the ragged prisoners disappeared.

"I don't know," said Tom. "If he finds out that we've escaped, we're in danger, too."

"We should find Silver and Storm quickly, then," said Elenna.

Tom peered round the moonlit square. There was no sign of anyone. The sun could rise at any moment, and then the villagers would be able to see them and attack.

"We need to find our weapons," Tom said. "Otherwise, we'll have to fight the Beast with our bare hands."

CHAPTER SIX

DANGER IN THE CORNFIELDS

Elenna pointed towards a low building at the side of the square. Harnesses hung from hooks on the wall. "It looks like a stable," she said.

As they walked towards the building, Tom heard a soft neigh from inside.

"Storm," he whispered, pushing open the rickety wooden door. Inside the building was a long corridor and a row of wooden stalls.

The stallion neighed again and Tom ran towards the sound. Storm was tied up in one of the stalls. Tom loosened the rope that fastened him to the manger.

"We'll get you out of here, right away," said Tom, as the black stallion rubbed his nose against his arm.

The straw piled in the corner was twitching and stirring. Silver poked his nose out from where he had been hiding after luring away the second guard. He jumped up and licked Elenna's hands. Then he started digging in the straw.

"He's found something," Elenna said, as Silver turned over a long piece of metal with his paws.

"My sword!" cried Tom. He buckled

the weapon around his waist. "Thank goodness this town has no armoury. This must have seemed like the best hiding place."

"It's nice to have some good fortune for a change," said Elenna.

Silver kept digging. Soon he had uncovered Tom's shield. Then Elenna knelt down and pulled out her bow and her quiver of arrows from under the manger.

She slung the quiver over her shoulder. "Now we can go on with the Quest."

"And it's more important than ever," Tom said. "Look what Velmal is doing to the people of this kingdom."

The four of them made their way out of the stable. As Tom pushed open the creaking wooden door, a bright ray of light struck his eyes.

The burning Kayonian sun was rising over the roofs of the houses. People were waking up!

Already Tom could see two men approaching. One brandished a long pitchfork with three deadly prongs. The other carried a sharp scythe. They cried out when they spotted Tom.

"There's no escape!" one shouted.

The men raced forwards. One swung his scythe at Tom's legs, the other lunged at Elenna with his pitchfork.

Tom leapt high in the air as the deadly blade whistled under his feet.

Elenna threw herself to the floor. The prongs of the fork shot over her, stabbing into a wooden pillar. Her attacker tugged at the handle, trying to free it. Elenna rolled towards him and grabbed him by the legs,

knocking him over.

Tom dodged another swipe from the scythe; the blade was so long he could not reach the villager with his sword.

There was a loud bark, and Silver bounded over to Tom's side. The fur on the back of his neck was standing up, and he growled angrily.

The villager turned his blue eyes to the wolf. Silver growled and stood firm. As the villager raised the scythe to slash at the wolf, Tom leapt from behind and brought his sword hilt down onto the back of the man's neck. He fell to the ground, dropping his weapon. Both the villagers were unconscious.

"We mustn't hurt them further," said Tom. "They only attacked us because Velmal has enchanted them."

Elenna ran to the stable and unhooked two long straps of leather from the wall. She used one of them to tie her captive's hands behind his back, and gave the other to Tom.

"We don't want these men shouting for help," she said, "I'll find something we can use as a gag."

"Good idea," said Tom. While he tied his prisoner's hands, Elenna went back to the stable and found an old rag. She tore it in half and tied a length around the prisoners' mouths.

With the two men shut up in the stable, Tom and Elenna headed for the fields, with Storm and Silver following close at their heels. The rotting cornstalks smelt vile as the friends pushed through them. Tom stumbled over a big piece of rusty metal.

"It's a farm implement," he said, "Just like the ploughs the farmers use in my village. But it's blunt and useless."

"There are broken tools everywhere," Elenna said. Hoes, spades and forks were lying discarded, all red with rust.

The one thing that did seem to be

working was the windmill. The sails were spinning smoothly, even though there was still no wind.

The stench of decay was getting stronger. It stung Tom's nose and made his head spin.

"The smell's worse near the windmill," he said.

"That's where it's coming from," said Elenna.

"Maybe it's part of Velmal's plan," said Tom, covering his nose with his hand. "It's a good way to keep intruders away. It makes me feel dizzy."

Elenna nodded. "Me too." She rubbed her forehead.

"We shouldn't stay here," said Tom. He looked around at the blackened cornstalks and the rusty implements lying uselessly on the ground. "The evil smell is helping Velmal to bewitch the villagers. And it's destroying everything – not just the crops, but these tools as well."

The friends pressed on, weaving their way through the rotten crops.

"What's that?" said Elenna, stopping in her tracks.

There was a crackling noise from the cornstalks, as if an army of creatures was on the march.

Tom gasped as a large rat sat up on its hind legs, glaring at Tom with its red eyes. It made a loud chattering noise and three other rats slid out from the cornstalks to join it.

It's calling to the others! Tom thought.

A flood of rats came pouring out of the corn in a squealing, dark torrent. Their high-pitched squeaks were like hundreds of unoiled door hinges, and their teeth gnashed hungrily.

CHAPTER SEVEN

THE RODENT ARMY

Tom had never seen so many rats. They scurried out from the rotting crops, advancing quickly towards him and Elenna.

"Urgh!" cried Elenna. The rats were scrambling over her feet and ankles.

Tom felt a nip on the back of his calf. "Ow!"

The rats squirmed up his legs,

crawling across his clothes and torso. *They're even bigger than the rats in King Hugo's dungeon*, he thought.

He could feel their claws digging into his flesh and their warm, furry bellies tickling his skin. Their whiskers trembled as they sniffed the air. A rat opened its mouth and sank long yellow teeth into Tom's shoulder.

"Get off!" Tom cried, angrily swatting the rat away. Streaks of his own blood stained his clothes as the rat flew over the corn.

Storm swished his tail, throwing off a rat that was hanging on. He stamped his hooves to repel the swarming creatures. Silver seized the rats one after the other in his strong jaws, flinging them high in the air.

Even that didn't stop them. With every passing second, more rats poured out of the corn. As soon as Tom got rid of a rat, two more jumped on him. "This means that the rat monster is somewhere nearby!" he cried.

Elenna didn't answer. A rat had jumped onto her shoulder and was biting her ear. She seized its tail and held it at arm's length. Its long whiskers quivered as it writhed upside down.

"Disgusting!" she said, dropping the rat back into the corn.

Suddenly, the rats stopped squeaking. Then, as swiftly as they had come, they scuttled away.

Elenna looked around. "Why did they go?" she asked.

"I don't know," said Tom. He felt

uneasy. "Maybe they're making way for something even bigger!"

"Let's check the map," said Elenna.

Tom pulled out the amulet.

"There we are," Elenna pointed at their position on the map, surrounded by the crops.

A menacing shape was travelling across the amulet's surface. "It's Muro!" Tom said.

The Beast was circling them. Though still some distance away, it got closer with every circle it made. Tom looked around the fields to try and spot the Beast, but his view was blocked by the dense cornstalks.

"I need to get higher," he said.

Storm was standing nearby. Tom grabbed the saddle and pulled himself into a standing position, balancing on Storm's stirrup.

"Can you make out anything?"
Elenna asked.

Tom strained his neck to see. All
around him, the harvest fields
stretched away like a golden ocean.
Somewhere, hidden under the
drooping ears of corn, the rat monster
was lurking; it must be very close now.
Silver growled softly, and Tom saw the
wolf lifting his muzzle to sniff the air.

"We have to get ready to fight,"
Tom said, dropping down from his
perch.

They needed space to defend
themselves. Tom drew his sword and
began to chop down the cornstalks,
creating enough room for him to
swing his blade, and Elenna to use
her bow.

A heat haze shimmered over the
crops. Tom stopped to wipe the sweat

from his brow. He was about to start chopping again when a savage screech split the air. The ground trembled with the rhythmic thud of heavy paws. A musty smell, like something left to rot for many years, drifted across the clearing that Tom had made.

Tom heard a horrible whistling, squeaking noise. He felt certain it was the Beast's panting breath. A swathe of cornstalks swirled, as if a great wind was stirring them.

Elenna nocked an arrow into her bow and Tom lifted his sword. As Muro's enormous body erupted into the clearing, Storm reared up and leapt sideways, disappearing into the corn. Silver dodged after him, the fur on his back bristling.

The Beast stopped dead. It crouched

in front of Tom, pawing the ground with its gnarled claws. From its evil rat's face, two stained incisors, sharp and deadly as pointed chisels, stabbed forward. The fur on its hunched back was filthy, with scabby patches of bare, wrinkled skin showing through. From its scaly cheeks, whiskers sprouted like stiff wires.

Tom shuddered. Long strings of drool dripped from the rat monster's mouth. Wherever the poisonous saliva fell, vegetation dissolved into stinking black liquid. Tom stared in horror as the Beast snorted its foul breath across the clearing.

Behind the Beast, a naked pink tail snaked, squirming with a life of its own. At the base of the tail was a green band. It looked like a ring made out of precious jade.

That must be the ingredient I need! Tom thought. Courage filled him as he realised that if he could claim the ring he would be one step nearer to saving his mother.

The ring cut deeply into the thick flesh of Muro's tail. It was so tight that Tom knew he would have to cut the tail right off to free the ring.

The Beast emitted a high-pitched shriek. Tom flinched as the sound rang in his ears; the cornstalks fell flat, as if a hurricane had hit them. Muro the rat monster charged.

CHAPTER EIGHT

AT THE MERCY OF THE BEAST

Elenna lifted her bow and loosed
an arrow at the Beast. The shaft
bounced off Muro's thick fur.

"Get out of the way!" Tom shouted,
struggling to make his voice heard
above the rat monster's horrible
shriek. He looked round for Storm
and Silver, but they had disappeared
into the corn.

Tom jumped sideways, pulling Elenna with him. They only just made it; as Muro careered off into the crops, one of its wiry whiskers lashed Tom's face.

"Tom, you're hurt!" Elenna said.

Tom touched his cheek and saw that his hand was covered in blood.

"Those whiskers are as sharp as knives," he said.

The cornfields were silent again. It was as if Muro had never been there. "Where did it go?" Elenna asked, her bow and arrow ready to shoot. "I don't know where to aim."

Before Tom could reply, there was another ear-splitting shriek. Muro exploded out of the corn and knocked Tom over, trampling him into the ground. Tom held his shield out for protection.

Muro's clawed paws crashed into
the shield, knocking the breath from
Tom's lungs. The Beast was trying to
crush him, but the shield held firm
against the attack.

The earth shook as Muro thundered away. Tom sat up. His head was spinning from the battering. There was no sign of the rat monster anywhere.

"Muro is playing with us," Tom said, as he got up. "It's acting like a cat, and we are the mice."

Another onslaught could come at any second. Tom repositioned his shield on his arm and clutched the hilt of his sword. The cornstalks shivered. Faster than ever, Muro burst out. Tom was ready. He sprang out of the Beast's path and, quick as a flash, he brought his sword down and sliced off one of Muro's whiskers.

Muro didn't slow down, and he vanished again. The whisker landed upright, as if it had been planted in the soil. Elenna reached out to take it. "I think I can use this," she said.

"Wrap some cloth round your hand," Tom said to her.

Elenna covered her hand with her scarf and drew the razor-edged whisker out of the soil. She tucked it into her quiver next to her arrows. Then she hid herself among the tall cornstalks.

The earth began to tremble. The rat monster bolted into the clearing, thick strings of drool flying from its jagged incisors. Its paws churned the black soil as it charged at Tom, flinging him down into the mud. Tom wriggled to escape. Then he heard Elenna's voice.

"I'm going to distract the Beast!" she called. "If we can get it between us, we have a better chance."

From her hiding place in the corn,

she whistled loudly. The rat monster swerved towards the sound. Its nose twitched and the razor-sharp whiskers trembled as it hunted Elenna.

Tom crawled as fast as he could through the mud until he rolled into a deep drainage ditch. The slimy water was disgusting. Tom caught his breath and struggled not to cough as the foul smell filled his lungs.

From the edge of the ditch he could see Elenna's bow peeping out from the cornstalks. She gave another whistle. As Muro charged, she lifted the bow and released, shooting their enemy with its own whisker. The Beast gave a shriek of agony as the dart pierced its hide.

Tom stood up, covered in stinking mud. He scrambled out of the ditch, making a loud squelching noise.

Muro swung round.

Tom's stomach churned. The time had come – he had to cut the ring from Muro's tail.

"While there's blood in my veins, I will defeat you!" Tom shouted.

The rat monster's tusk-like teeth snapped with rage, and steaming saliva fell from its mouth.

"Look out!" called Elenna. She fitted an arrow into her bow and loosed it. The shaft glanced off Muro's hide.

Tom stood at the edge of the clearing, and braced himself for the attack. But Muro hesitated, twitching his nose.

The Beast lumbered across the clearing. Its head swung from side to side. Now the deadly incisors were just a foot away from Tom's legs. He was just about to slash at the

rat monster with his sword when the
Beast stopped dead.

Why doesn't it charge? Tom thought.
I'm right in front of it!

Muro peered at Tom. Its red eyes
were covered with a pale, whitish
film. Back in Tom's village, one of

the old villagers had a similar white veil over his eyes. That man was blind.

Tom waved his sword in front of Muro's face. The Beast did not respond.

The rat monster couldn't see!

CHAPTER NINE

BATTLE OF THE WINDMILL

Tom's heart thudded as he waved
to Elenna. He covered his eyes and
pointed to Muro, signalling that the
Beast was blind. She nodded, keeping
her arrow trained on the Beast.

Tom crept towards the ditch. Muro
stood in the centre of the clearing, its
nose twitching. *Why doesn't it follow me?*
thought Tom as he slid into the ditch.

The putrid stench of the stagnant, muddy water filled his nostrils.

Now Tom understood! The stinking mud that covered his clothes was masking his smell! The rat monster was snuffling around the edge of the clearing. Tom crept to Elenna's hiding place.

"Quick," he hissed, "get down in here!"

Elenna looked doubtful. "It smells disgusting," she said.

"That's the idea," Tom whispered. "I'm covered in smelly mud. That's why Muro can't find me."

Elenna climbed into the ditch and plastered black mud over herself. The Beast left the clearing, tracking through the crops as it hunted for them. Tom and Elenna clambered out of the ditch, mud and water dripping from their clothes.

The cornstalks stirred with a whispering sound. Tom's heart jumped. He was ready to dive back into the ditch when he saw Storm and Silver, cautiously peering out.

Tom listened hard. There was no sound of Muro's return.

"I'm going to creep up on the Beast and get the ring from its tail," he told Elenna. "Follow me and keep a lookout."

They trod softly over the dry, crunching stalks. Soon Tom heard the whistling of the rat monster's breath. Pushing the corn aside, he spied Muro just a few paces away. The Beast's blind eyes blinked.

He's confused, thought Tom, and he felt a sliver of sympathy for the Beast. Tom shuffled forwards. In front of him, Muro's bald tail snaked along the ground. Tom crept forwards; there was a loud *crack* as he stepped on a brittle shaft of corn.

Muro's head turned. The massive Beast lurched towards Tom, its scabby body scraping through the corn.

Tom was trapped! Muro's head hit him in the stomach. Tom gasped as he flew up in the air. He landed astride the rat monster, facing his tail.

The Beast bucked like an angry bull. Tom dug his heels in and Muro roared with rage. It kicked its hind legs, rolling Tom backwards over its neck. Then it reared up, wheeling its front paws and Tom was thrown towards the tail.

Through the blur, Tom saw Elenna drawing back her bow.

"Keep away!" Tom shouted. The

Beast spun round, screaming with fury as it heard Tom's voice.

Tom clung on. He could see the jade ring – it was close enough to touch. If he could cut through Muro's tail the prize would be his; but the Beast was bucking so hard that he needed both hands to hold on to its fur.

Muro seemed to know what Tom was trying to do. The Beast twitched its tail like a whip. Muro's evil jaws swung round and Tom cried out in pain as the teeth caught his leg. One of Elenna's arrows hit Muro's face. The Beast squealed, releasing its grip on Tom's calf.

Tom swivelled round on the Beast's back so he could see where they were going. Muro charged off into the lashing cornstalks, but Tom hung on with his knees and hands.

"I'll stick with you until you drop!" he shouted to the Beast.

Muro shrieked and sped onwards towards the village.

The windmill! Tom thought. *If only I can force Muro over there!*

Tom grabbed the rat monster's mangy fur, pulling its neck to steer the racing Beast. Muro twisted and turned, trying to escape Tom's painful tugs.

The brick windmill loomed before them. Tom urged the blind Beast on, lifting his legs to plant his feet on Muro's back. Any second… *Now!*

Tom leapt into the air, somersaulting backwards. He heard an almighty *crunch* as the Beast collided into the building. Muro collapsed into a heap. After a moment, the twitching stopped and the rat monster was still.

I've done it! thought Tom. *The Beast is vanquished!*

The windmill's sails were broken. He took a deep breath – at last the air was clear!

There was just one thing left to do: get the ring. Tom drew his sword, ready to chop off Muro's tail.

Thwack! Something hit him across the back. Tom staggered from the blow. When he looked up, he saw one of the blue-eyed villagers standing over him, brandishing a knotted branch.

The rat monster staggered to its feet. Tom's heart sank as it stumbled into the cornfields, the jade ring still attached to its tail. He could not follow. Other villagers were arriving, carrying scythes and sticks. Tom's blood ran cold as he heard a cackle of laughter from the sky above his head.

"Well, Tom!" Velmal's cruel voice echoed like thunder. "The end has come. Prepare to meet your fate!"

CHAPTER TEN

THE JADE RING

Tom was surrounded. A shiver ran down his spine as the blue-eyed villagers stared at him. With Velmal's evil coursing through them, Tom knew they would show no mercy.

The villagers pinned his arms and threatened him with rusty knives.

"Go, boy, go!" Elenna shouted. With a thunder of hooves, Tom's stallion galloped at the villagers with

Elenna sat tall in the saddle. Silver raced alongside, his teeth bared in a snarl.

The villagers scattered before them. Elenna reached down and Tom grabbed her hand. He pulled himself up to sit behind her on Storm's back.

"We have to get the ring!" Tom shouted as Storm galloped into the cornfields, following the trail of stalks flattened by the fleeing rat monster. All was quiet. Tom felt frustration boiling up inside him. "Muro has outwitted us," he said.

Silver gave a low growl.

"He'll find Muro," Elenna said. "Seek the Beast, Silver!"

Silver dived into the corn.

Tom and Elenna waited, staring out over the crops. At last, the sound of distant barking rose up in the hot air. Silver had found something. Moments later, he returned. Behind him, shaking the ground with its enormous paws, came Muro.

Storm snorted. The Beast shrieked at the sound and lowered its head to charge. But Storm was too quick; as

the Beast strode forward, the stallion
leapt out of the way.

It was the moment Tom had been
waiting for. As the rat monster
thundered past, Tom jumped down
and with one swift blow he cut the
tail clean off.

A choking roar escaped from
Muro's lips. The Beast slid to a halt.

Its massive body was shrinking, crumbling away. In its place, hundreds of tiny grey-brown rats now ran about, chittering and squeaking.

"We did it!" Tom shouted, lifting the heavy tail.

The villagers were approaching across the fields.

"Trait—" one of them began to cry out. Then his voice dried up in his throat. The villagers stopped. One of them announced in a shaky voice: "The boy has defeated Muro. He's… He's a hero…" Tom could see the villagers blinking, as if they'd just woken up. The whites of their eyes shone again and they looked confused.

Tom raised his hands. "Dark magic is powerful. But you're free now. Go back to your lives."

The villagers nodded, murmuring thanks and good wishes as they walked back to their village.

Tom pulled at the gleaming jade ring. It slid easily off the rat monster's severed tail. "Let's head for the village," he said to Elenna. His heart swelled with pride as he thought of the bravery she and their animal companions had shown.

In the village square, a skinny figure wearing a wizard's hat was squatting beside a cauldron. It was Marc.

"Tom and Elenna! Well done," he called. "You have completed your Quest!" Marc put his hand up to his nose. "Phew," he said. "I think you need a bath!" He stared at Tom and Elenna's filthy clothes.

Tom grinned. "Lucky there's a pump here," he said. He pulled the handle. It was still jammed.

Aduro's apprentice tapped the pump with his wand and a fountain of bubbling water gushed out. The villagers came running over. Elenna grabbed a mug and began pouring water for them. The people drank thirstily from their cupped hands.

One of the villagers wiped his mouth and turned to address his friends.

"The curse is lifted!"

"We're free!" another villager cried. Soon all the men and women were smiling. They came up to Tom and Elenna and thanked them.

The man who had held Elenna captive earlier spoke. "We've work to do," he said. "There are still healthy crops to harvest. Let us go!"

Tom and Marc watched the villagers tramping off into the fields, chatting and laughing.

Marc spoke to Tom. "The warrior queen is very grateful for the men that you sent to her," he said. "Every person counts in our struggle against Velmal."

"Those men were imprisoned for stealing," Tom said. "They did wrong. But there are far greater evils happening in Kayonia. We've got to keep fighting until Velmal is defeated."

Marc nodded. "Let's add the next ingredient to the potion," he said.

Tom gave him the jade ring, and Marc dropped it into the cauldron.

"Remember, Tom," he said. "This potion, which will save your mother from her sickness, is still far from complete. The jade ring will restore Freya's strength, but there are still four more ingredients to find."

Tom's heart felt heavy. Was his mother even still alive?

"Are you up to this, Tom?" Marc asked him. "Your toughest Quest awaits you. You must face Fang the bat fiend."

Tom did not hesitate. He gripped his sword hilt. Elenna, Storm and Silver were close by his side. There was no way Tom was going to shirk the challenge.

"While there's blood in my veins," he cried, "Velmal will never take my mother's life!"

Here's a sneak preview of Tom's
next exciting adventure!

Meet

FanG
THE BAT FIEND

Only Tom can free the Beasts from
Velmal's wicked enchantment...

PROLOGUE

Toby grasped his pickaxe, wincing at the pain from his blistered hands. He could hardly see the wall in front of him. Frustration at his dim sight swept over him and he attacked the rockface even harder than usual. As he swung the pickaxe, the blows echoed off the wall, blending with the strokes of the other workers beside him and the clink of the chains that bound them.

*More gold...*Toby thought wearily. More riches flowing like a river through the Golden Valley of Kayonia.

Pausing to ease his aching shoulders, he listened to the grunts and groans of his fellow slaves.

They're all content to be blind. Just as long as their town has wealth. Toby gripped his axe harder, as if he wanted to break the handle. *But I'm not content...*

"Here, what do you think you're doing?"

Toby jumped at the whispering voice of Jed, the man working next to him. "Get back to work, or the master will punish you."

Toby's anger wrestled with his fear. "I don't care!" he declared, standing up straight. "I'm sick of being a slave. I'm going to break free of this place! Who's with me?"

There was no reply, except for the renewed hammering of pickaxes. Toby could feel the fear of the other slaves; they were acting like he wasn't there. He understood why they were scared. Their master seemed to move about them in total silence, until he announced himself with echoing shrieks and screeches that made Toby's ears hurt.

"Don't be a fool," Jed said in a low voice. Toby could hardly see him swing his pickaxe, because of his poor eyesight. "You can't escape. The master's not like us. He can see in the dark, for one thing. He could be watching us, right now..."

Follow this Quest to the end in FANG THE BAT FIEND.

Win an exclusive
Beast Quest T-shirt and goody bag!

Tom has battled many fearsome Beasts and we want to know which one is your favourite! Send us a drawing or painting of your favourite Beast and tell us in 30 words why you think it's the best.

Each month we will select **three** winners to receive a Beast Quest T-shirt and goody bag!

Send your entry on a postcard to
BEAST QUEST COMPETITION
Orchard Books, 338 Euston Road, London NW1 3BH.

Australian readers should email:
childrens.books@hachette.com.au

New Zealand readers should write to:
Beast Quest Competition, 4 Whetu Place, Mairangi Bay, Auckland NZ, or email: childrensbooks@hachette.co.nz

**Don't forget to include your name and address.
Only one entry per child.**

Good luck!

Join the Quest,
Join the Tribe

www.beastquest.co.uk

Have you checked out the Beast Quest website?
It's the place to go for games, downloads, activities,
sneak previews and lots of fun!

You can read all about your favourite Beasts, down-
load free screensavers and desktop wallpapers for
your computer, and even challenge your friends
to a Beast Tournament.

Sign up to the newsletter at www.beastquest.co.uk
to receive exclusive extra content and the oppor-
tunity to enter special members-only competitions.
We'll send you up-to-date info on all the Beast
Quest books, including the next exciting series
which features six brand-new Beasts!

Get 30% off all Beast Quest Books at www.beastquest.co.uk
Enter the code BEAST at the checkout.

All books priced at £4.99.
Special bumper editions priced at £5.99.

Orchard Books are available from all good bookshops, or can
be ordered from our website: www.orchardbooks.co.uk,
or telephone 01235 827702, or fax 01235 8227703.

FREE COLLECTOR CARDS INSIDE!

Series 6

 BEAST QUEST

Can Tom and his companions rescue his mother
from the clutches of evil Velmal...?

978 1 40830 723 6

978 1 40830 724 3

978 1 40830 725 0

978 1 40830 726 7

978 1 40830 727 4

978 1 40830 728 1

978 1 40830 735 9

Does Tom have the
strength to triumph
over cunning Creta?

Series 11: THE NEW AGE
COLLECT THEM ALL!

A new land, a deadly enemy and six new Beasts await Tom on his next adventure!

978 1 40831 841 6

978 1 40831 842 3

978 1 40831 843 0

978 1 40831 844 7

978 1 40831 845 4

978 1 40831 846 1